Ruby Rogers
is a Walking Legend

Ruby Rogers
is a Walking Legend

Sue Limb

Illustrations by Bernice Lum

BLOOMSBURY

To Roger (my evil older bro)

First published in Great Britain in 2007 by Bloomsbury Publishing Plc
36 Soho Square, London, WID 3QY

Text copyright © Sue Limb 2007
Illustrations copyright © Bernice Lum 2007
The moral rights of the author and illustrator have been asserted

A CIP catalogue record of this book is available from the British Library

ISBN 978 0 7475 8323 3

All papers used by Bloomsbury Publishing are natural, recyclable
products made from wood grown in well-managed forests.
The manufacturing processes conform to the environmental
regulations of the country of origin.

Printed in Great Britain by Clays Ltd, St Ives Plc

1 3 5 7 9 10 8 6 4 2

www.suelimbbooks.co.uk
www.bloomsbury.com

CHAPTER 1

There's nothing to be scared of!

I TEXTED YASMIN: *THERE IS SOME-THING EVIL UP IN MY BEDROOM, SO I AM SITTING ON THE STAIRS, POSSIBLY FOR THE REST OF MY LIFE.* There was no reply. Her dad is really strict and she has to go to bed early and leave her mobile downstairs. Otherwise we'd probably text each other all night under the bedclothes. And if we could do that, maybe I wouldn't get so scared.

Mum and Dad were watching a wildlife programme.

5

Joe was up in his room, working. Sometimes he's got loud music on, but tonight it was quiet. Horribly quiet. I'd been on my way upstairs to go to bed when I heard a sound. A sort of rustle. Coming from my bedroom, not Joe's. It wasn't Joe moving about in his room. It was something evil moving about in mine.

My blood went cold. The wildlife programme on TV was making some really weird sounds. Howler monkeys were howling in the depths of the rainforest. A bird gave a sudden eerie cry. Goosebumps came up on my arms and legs. It had been dark for hours. I hate this time of year.

'I so *love* this time of year!' Yasmin says, kicking the autumn leaves about. 'Hallowe'en and Bonfire Night, and Christmas! And the school play!' Yasmin's playing Princess Jasmine in *Aladdin*: a starring role. I've got a tiny part. It's only a few lines but I'm still nervous. It's ridiculous, I know, being scared of the school play. But I am kind of jumpy this time of year. When I was really little I was even scared of Father Christmas. And most of all I'm scared of the dark.

Nobody must ever know what a scaredy-cat I am, because I'm supposed to be hard and cool. I want to be a gangster when I grow up.

'Ruby!' Mum came out of the sitting room suddenly. So suddenly it made me jump. 'Why aren't you in bed? What are you doing there?'

'I thought I heard a noise upstairs,' I said.

'Don't be silly, love. There's nothing to be afraid of! Up you go!' Mum bustled off to the kitchen and put the kettle on. I followed her. It was so cosy in there. If only I could sleep on the kitchen floor, like a dog in a basket. They could even call me Rover. I wouldn't mind.

'Mum,' I said. 'Please – just come up with me.'

The phone rang. Mum answered it. It was Granny. Mum sat down in a chair, pulled a 'bor-*ing*' face and started to listen. I knew this call would take for ever. Granny talks non-stop about her cat, Horace. Mum was nodding and listening, but she glared at me and pointed fiercely to the clock and then the door.

The message was clear: go to bed or there will be big trouble, possibly involving shouting. Mum can be fierce. When she shouts, sometimes a little bit of spit comes flying out of her mouth. But you mustn't laugh or she gets even crosser.

I went out into the hall. I could hear the adverts on TV. I edged my way into the sitting room. Dad had his sock off and was examining his big toe.

'Dad,' I said, 'please could you take me up to bed? I'm scared.'

'*You're* scared?' said Dad. 'I think I'm getting arthritis in my big toe. This is a disaster. I'm only forty. My dad didn't get it till he was sixty. This is so unfair.'

He did go upstairs with me, though. We went into my bedroom and he switched the main light on. It looked completely normal. Dad sat down on my little stool and put his sock back on again.

'Off you go to bed, then,' he said.

'But I haven't done my teeth or got my pyjamas on yet,' I said.

'Well, get a move on,' said Dad. 'I want to get back to the howler monkeys.'

He picked up one of my *Harry Potter* books and started to read it. I raced to the bathroom, did my teeth and dived into my PJs.

Then I rushed back to my room. Dad pulled a face at the *Harry Potter* book and put it back on the shelf.

'No wonder you're a bag of nerves,' he said. 'I've only been reading it for two minutes and I'm scared to death.'

'Dad!' I said. 'You shouldn't say things like that! Dads should be calm and reassuring.'

'Sorry,' said Dad. 'I forgot. Now, up you go to bed, Rube. Giss a kiss – I'm not climbing up that contraption. I've got no head for heights.'

I gave Dad a kiss and a hug, and then climbed up my stepladder to my tree-house platform, where I sleep. It's the most fantastic thing. All my friends are *so* envious of me having a tree house in my bedroom and sleeping up in the branches instead of in a boring ordinary bed.

My monkeys were already in bed, and they got a bit grumpy when I grabbed the best pillow. They're supposed to be my toys, but sometimes they behave as if they own the place.

'Night-night then, lovey!' said Dad, standing by the door. He switched the light off.

'Night, Dad!' Dad closed the door and went downstairs. For an instant everything seemed pitch black. But then my eyes got used to the dark, and the shape of the window became clear with the streetlights shining in through the curtains.

I closed my eyes and started to try to get to sleep. But I felt wide awake. I thought I heard stealthy foot-steps: *tread, tread, tread*. Then I realised it was my own pulse beating in my ear. I sat up and punched the pillows a bit, trying to get more comfortable.

'For cryin' out loud!' said Stinker (he's the boss monkey). 'Give us a break!'

I lay down again. I closed my eyes. I tried to count sheep. Then I tried to count monkeys.

Then I heard it: *breathing*. Instantly my whole body tensed. Maybe it was my own breathing. I held my breath. The breathing went on and on. Big, heavy breaths – the sort of breathing a mon-ster would do. I wasn't imagining it! There *was* something evil in my room!

I was just about to scream for help, when I heard another sound. A faint scratching and a horrible, blood-curdling moan ... and it was definitely com-ing from my wardrobe!

CHAPTER 2
You're an evil monster!

I SAT BOLT UPRIGHT, my pulse racing.
The wardrobe door twitched for a split second.
Then, very, very slowly, it *swung open*.

Had the door just opened by itself, sort of by
accident? Had it not been closed properly?
(When did I ever close it properly?) Oh, why had-
n't Mum come upstairs with me? Mum would
have insisted on hanging my clothes up in the
wardrobe. Dad hadn't even noticed where I'd
chucked them.

If only I'd hung my clothes up just now, I'd

know for sure that there was absolutely nobody and nothing in the wardrobe.

The door still hung open. There was silence. My heartbeat began to slow. Maybe it was just one of those odd spooky moments after all, when objects seem to do weird stuff on their own.

Then, slowly, and with a terrible quietness, a figure *stepped out of the wardrobe*. It was a hunched figure, short and stocky, and in the darkness it looked as if it had no head. *No head!* I opened my mouth to scream, but no sound came out. I was paralysed, like in a bad dream.

Some kind of sickening dwarf! A horrible mon-sterish thing was actually *in my bedroom*. It must be a dream, it must be a dream! I stretched my eyes wide, the way I always do when I know I'm having a nightmare and want to wake up. But it didn't work. I was wide awake – and the thing was really there, creeping in a hideous way towards the foot of my ladder!

Then, suddenly, I noticed something. I could smell Joe's aftershave. Since he started going out with the irritating Tiffany, Joe's been splashing something called Stag all over his neck every evening – even though he only shaves once a week. This horrible headless monster had got to be Joe! Typical!

My terror changed into fury. I hated him for this. He had scared me half to death. And now he was climbing up the ladder to my private tree house! Climbing up in an evil way, in his stockinged feet, with his fleece pulled up right over his head so he looked like a Headless Horror!

Swiftly I looked around for something to hit him with. Just to the side of my mattress there's a little built-in shelf for books and stuff. And there was a big glass of water. I grabbed it, and just as the Joe-monster reached the top of the ladder, I hurled

the water down inside the open neck of the fleece.

'Aaaargh!' spluttered the Joe-monster. I reached down inside the neck of the fleece and grabbed a handful of his wet hair. I pulled with all my might. 'Owwwwww!' roared Joe. He lashed out wildly to try and make me let go, but of course, with his head buried deep in his fleece, he couldn't see. He lost his balance and fell off the ladder on to the floor.

There was a terrific thud. The room actually *shook*. I jumped down the ladder, grabbed my tennis racket and let Joe have what he deserved: forehand, backhand, volley. Joe struggled to his feet, roaring, his head still buried.

'Cut it out!' yelled Joe, staggering about and trying to get his head out of his fleece.

'Why should I?' I yelled, whacking him with all my strength. 'You're an evil monster!'

Joe managed to unzip the neck of his fleece and his head popped out. He grabbed the tennis racket, half-breaking my wrist. I screamed.

The door flew open and the light snapped on. Mum stood there, her eyes flashing.

'What's going on?' she shouted. 'For goodness's sake! The ceiling's shaking down in the room below!'

'Joe hid in my wardrobe!' I yelled. 'He waited till my light was out, then he came out and scared me! He was disguised as a horrible headless monster!'

'Joe, get out!' snapped Mum, taking the tennis racket off him.

Joe slithered passed her. He hissed briefly at me as he went, like a snake. This is his usual way of saying, 'You're a sneak!' I ignored him.

Mum closed the door behind him and propped the tennis racket up by the wall.

'Get up that ladder to bed!' she said grumpily.

'There's no need to be cross with me!' My temper flared again. 'I just went to bed and he was hiding in my wardrobe all the time! Disguised as an evil headless monster!'

'Don't exaggerate, Ruby,' said Mum, looking tired. 'He looked perfectly normal.'

'He had his fleece pulled up over his head!' I said. 'He was like a headless ghost or something!'

Mum smiled. Normally I'd be pleased if she smiled. But this time it was infuriating. It seemed as if she was on Joe's side, enjoying his joke.

'He frightened me to death!' I screamed, climbing up my ladder. 'You don't care! You just think it's funny! It wasn't! It was horrible! It was the most horrible moment of my life!'

'Calm down, now, Ruby,' said Mum. 'Give me a kiss.' She climbed up the ladder a bit.

'No!' I said, throwing myself down on the mattress and pulling up the duvet round my shoulders. I lay out of reach, with my face turned away from Mum. 'Joe plays a horrible evil trick on me, and all you can do is laugh! Go away!'

There was a pause, and then Mum went down the ladder again. She walked to the door.

'I'm going to give him a severe talking to, right now,' she said softly. 'Now you get some sleep, or you'll be too tired for school in the morning.'

'That's all I ever wanted to do anyway!' I snapped. 'How am I ever going to get to sleep after that? I'll have nightmares!'

'Shall I leave the light on, then?' asked Mum.

'Do what you like! I don't care!' I yelled, and pulled the bedclothes up right over my head.

Mum left the light on and shut the door. I heard her going to Joe's room next door, and the sound of voices. Mum didn't sound nearly angry enough with him. He's the favourite. I know he is. Everybody loves him, and nobody loves me.

I clutched my monkeys in my arms and tried to cry. I managed a few tears, but then Stinker started to fidget.

'Hey!' he complained. 'A guy can't breathe like dis! Give us some air, can'tcha?' I loosened my grip.

'Dat's better,' said Stinker. 'And stop ya caterwauling. Don't get sad, get even!'

Stinker was right. Tears were for sissies. What I needed wasn't a cry. It was *revenge*.

CHAPTER 3
What's the matter, Ruby?

'WE'RE HAVING A run-through of *Aladdin* this morning,' Miss Jenkins announced. Her eyebrows were blacker than ever today, and her eyes were glittery and fierce. 'We're getting together with Mr Rivers' class in the hall. All right, get up and walk to the hall quietly – *quietly!* And in single file!'

'Brilliant! Brilliant!' whispered Yasmin, as we marched along. 'Thank God I went through my lines last night!'

'Wicked!' said Dan in his wicked voice. He's playing the evil villain, Abanazer. Dan is my best boy friend. I call him 'Froggo' because of his rather goggly eyes and wide smile. Max is playing Aladdin. He's not brilliant but he *is* tall.

Everybody knows the story about Aladdin and his magic lamp. He rubs it and out pops the genie. The genie's being played by a big girl called Sophie Percival. It all starts in a laundry. There are loads of people playing laundry workers. The chief two are Wishee Washee and Hanky Panky. My part is Wishee Washee.

I only have a couple of lines, and one verse of a song, but I was already feeling sick with nerves when we arrived in the school hall. Mr Rivers took us round backstage and gave us a little pep talk.

'You all know your lines by now,' he said. 'This is just a chance for you to get a feel of how the whole play runs along. It'll give you an idea of where your scenes come and how important it is to *listen* to what's happening on stage.

'I shall be *totally furious,*' he added, grinning – he's such a lovely teacher, not like Jenko – 'if anybody misses their cue because they're gassing to their friends backstage. Once you know the moment has come for you to go onstage, just get on and sharpish! You'll have to keep your wits about you. So there's a strict rule backstage of absolutely *no talking whatever.* OK?'

We nodded. None of us was going to miss our cue. Everybody adores Mr Rivers. I've never seen him totally furious, but he has been a bit upset a few times and that was awful – worse than if an ordinary teacher had been 'totally furious'.

The audience settled down out in the hall with Mrs Jenkins. We took our places in the wings, on either side of the stage, in the dark. Mr Rivers was standing at a stage manager's desk, kind of hidden at the side of the stage, behind the curtains. He was working the lights or something. He pressed a button and some Oriental music started, and the lights went up. The first person onstage was Max, as Aladdin.

Max landed on stage with a tremendous bound, and went into his first speech. He gabbled a bit, but he did remember his words. Still, I didn't have time to think about Max's performance. I was so terrified about my own. In a few minutes' time it would be my cue – time for me to run onstage, looking for Hanky Panky. As my cue got nearer and nearer my heart beat faster and faster, until the sickening moment when Froggo, as the evil Abanazer, finished his speech and disappeared in a swirl of blackness on the other side of the stage.

Now was the moment! I had to go! I rushed onstage, almost tripping over my feet, and looked around frantically. Thank goodness I had so few lines. There was no problem about remembering my words. All I had to say was 'Hanky Panky!' I opened my mouth. It felt dry. All the faces in the audience looking at me were a sea of pink.

'Happy Pancake!' I shouted. Oh Lordy! What had I said? It was wrong, rubbish! People in the audience giggled. 'Happy – Panky!' I tried again. My voice sounded weedy and quivery. I hated myself for being such an idiot. Everybody laughed again.

'Happy . . . Hanky Panky!' I shouted, finally getting it right. I went bright red. It had been a terrible feeling when the audience laughed at me. I'd felt totally stupid. At last Hanky Panky arrived on stage – a boy with ginger hair, called Owen. We got on with our scene. Having to concentrate on the next bit kind of blotted out the awful moment when I hadn't been able to remember Hanky Panky's name.

Afterwards we joined the audience in the hall and all sat on the floor while Mr Rivers talked about the performance. He seemed really pleased, and he didn't mention the time when I'd got Hanky Panky's name wrong. But I knew I'd be haunted by it for the whole of the rest of my *life*.

'Wasn't the run-through brilliant?' said Yasmin at lunchtime. 'I can't wait for the real thing, with all the costumes and everything.' Yasmin's costume is going to be wonderful: harem pants and a glittery shrug all covered with sequins. And shoes with pointy, curled-up toes. And she's going to have her hair up, with butterflies on it. 'Imagine how fantastic it'll be to do the play at night!' she said. 'With a huge audience of grown-ups, all the parents and stuff. My granny's coming over from Turkey to see it!'

This was bad news. Last time I'd seen Yasmin's granny, she'd practically broken my neck with an over-enthusiastic hug. But Yasmin's granny's hugs were nothing compared to the awful thought of doing the play in front of a huge audience of grown-ups, for real. I seriously considered the possibility of running away.

After school, I was walking home rather gloomily, when I heard somebody call my name. I turned round and there was Holly Helvellyn! The divine Holly! I grinned as she strolled up. She was looking *sooo* cool in black and purple, with black net gloves and bits of metal everywhere.

'You look like a girl who needs a peanut,' said

Holly, offering me one. I accepted eagerly. I hadn't eaten much lunch – I'd felt sick after that horrible run-through. 'You shouldn't eat too much salted stuff,' said Holly, 'so this is my last packet. What's the matter, Ruby?'

I told her all·about the awful fool I'd made of myself this morning in the run-through. And then I told her about Joe playing that horrid trick on me last night. I wondered if Holly still fancied Joe, despite the fact that stinky old Tiffany was still hanging round him. I hoped Holly still *did* fancy Joe. I hadn't completely given up hope of getting them together.

'So, he pretended to be a headless monster and frightened you to death?' said Holly. If she wanted to laugh, she certainly didn't show it. Instead she threw the salted-nut packet into a litter bin and linked arms with me. 'Hmmmmm,' said Holly. 'I don't blame you for feeling a bit down – mind that dog poo!'

She pulled me fiercely to one side, avoiding the dreaded doo-doo by centimetres. I so hate it when people let their dogs do that. If I had a dog, I'd . . . Well, if I had a dog, it would have to wear nappies.

'Things could be worse, though,' said Holly. 'Imagine if you'd trodden in it. In fact, imagine if you were a girl who'd just trodden in dog poo, and you were being chased by a lion.'

'Yes . . .' I thought for a minute. 'And imagine this girl . . . What shall we call her?'

'Agatha Widebottom,' said Holly. I grinned.

'Imagine a snake had laid its eggs inside Agatha's pocket,' I said, 'and they were just about to hatch.'

'Imagine a snake had laid its eggs in her *nostril*,' said Holly. I gave a shriek of lovely horror.

'Imagine she looked down and saw grass growing out of her legs,' I said, remembering a nightmare I'd had once.

'Getting very Gothic now, aren't we?' said Holly. 'And what if Agatha got home, and found her mum had turned into a vampire, and her dad had turned into a werewolf.'

'What about her brother?' I asked, watching Holly carefully.

'Oh, nothing much had happened to her brother,' laughed Holly. 'He was so totally revolting already, he couldn't possibly have been worse. Those pulsating green warts on his nose!'

I laughed. Suddenly we were at my house. Time always flew past when Holly was with me.

'Come in and have tea!' I begged.

'Sorry, Rube, can't today,' said Holly. 'Have stuff to do.'

'Will you babysit for me next Friday?' I asked. 'Mum and Dad are going out.'

'I'll have a look at my diary when I get home,' said Holly. 'Ring me and we'll talk about it, OK?'

She gave me a kiss and walked off down the road, jingling faintly. I stood and watched for a moment. Holly was amaaaaaaazing. I couldn't wait to see her again.

CHAPTER 4
What's all that mess?

I LET MYSELF INTO the house. Usually Joe arrives back from school around the same time as me, but there was no sign of him. Dad hadn't got back home either. He's a geography teacher, so he sometimes forgets where we live. Mum's a midwife, so she works different shifts and sometimes she's waiting at home for me with a lovely hot meal. But not today.

It was such a gloomy afternoon – almost dark already. I immediately ran round the ground floor, switching on all the lights. I turned the TV on too.

I was going to watch *The Simpsons* until another member of my useless family arrived to keep me company.

If only Holly had come in with me. That was my stupid family's fault too. Joe! What a waste of space! If only he hadn't upset Holly by seeming interested in her and then ignoring her and going off with that no-brain Tiffany! Then Holly would be right here with me, being a sort of older sister – something I've always wanted. But, as my parents have explained many times, it's a bit too late for an older sister now.

I went into the kitchen. It was bright and cheerful in there. I wasn't going upstairs until somebody else came home. In the fridge was my favourite

yogurt: raspberry. I chopped up a banana into a bowl and tipped my favourite yogurt all over it and stirred it up. Then I shook a few chopped nuts on top. I got a big glass and poured myself some tropical fruit juice. Then I carried my lovely snack into the sitting room.

Before I sat down, though, I was going to close those curtains. It was so gloomy and murky outside, it was almost dark. Still carrying my snack, I approached the window that looks out on to the back garden – and suddenly my heart almost shot clean out of my chest!

There were two hideous ugly faces squashed up against the glass! The banana'n'yogurt dish flew out of my hand. The tropical fruit juice hit the ceiling. My heart performed two circuits of the room and came to rest in a bowl of fruit.

But the terror only lasted a couple of seconds. One of the faces started to grin and vibrate, and moved away from the glass, and I could hear Tiffany laughing her snorting piggy laugh.

The other face was still pressed up against the window, and it was making a growling noise. Of course, it was Joe. I drew the curtains right across to hide him and marched off to the kitchen to get a bucket of water and a cloth, because, thanks to my idiot brother and his girlfriend from hell, the carpet was a total mess.

The pud was scattered over a wide area. I managed to scrape it back into the bowl, and scrubbed the stains on the carpet. Joe and Tiffany came in.

'Oh sorreee we made you jump so much, Rube!' cackled Tiffany. 'But it was soooooo funny!'

I ignored her. They plonked themselves down on the sofa and Joe surfed through the channels until he found something more to his taste than *The Simpsons*. It was some stupid martial arts movie. *The Simpsons* is way too intelligent for him.

I finished scrubbing the carpet and then carried the bucket and the plate of banana'n'yogurt'n'carpet fluff back to the kitchen. Obviously, I wasn't going to eat it. But I had a little idea.

Quietly I took it upstairs. The movie was so loud, Joe and Tiffany would never hear me. I tiptoed along the landing, past my own bedroom door and very carefully entered Joe's bedroom.

I didn't even switch the light on – I could see my way in the faint gloom. I crept to his bed, pulled back the duvet and tipped the pudding out slap-bang in the middle of his bed. Then I replaced the duvet, went back downstairs and put the empty bowl in the dishwasher.

After that I went up to my room and spent some quality time in my tree house with the monkeys. I couldn't wait for Joe to come upstairs and be disgusted. But of course, he stayed downstairs with Tiffany. I heard Mum come in and ask, 'Where's Ruby?'

'She's sulking in her room,' said Joe. 'I had to tell her off for making a mess. Girl Drops Snack – Priceless Carpet Ruined.'

'Oh, no!' said Mum. 'Look at that, now!'

I was so tempted to burst out of my room, rush downstairs and throw myself at Joe. I *so* longed to gouge his eyes out, pull out whole handfuls of his hair or possibly sink my teeth into his leg and never let go. But knowing Tiffany was there made it different. I wasn't going to lose my dignity in front of her – again. It was bad enough that she'd seen me hurling puddings about in panic.

I wasn't going to speak to Tiffany again as long as I lived, even if she married Joe. I might pass her a note at Christmas. It would say: *Happy Christmas and Get Outta My Face!*

Mum's footsteps came upstairs. She came straight into my room. I was sitting up on my tree-house platform, so I felt kind of safe and out of reach.

'What's all that mess on the sitting-room carpet, Ruby?' she demanded.

'I was just carrying a little snack into the room,' I said, 'and Joe and Tiffany were hiding out in the garden and they pressed their faces up against the glass and it made me jump so much I dropped everything.'

'How many times do I have to tell you?' sighed Mum. 'Snacks at the kitchen table, not in front of the TV!' She's fighting a losing battle, though. Even she and Dad have fish and chips in front of the telly sometimes on a Saturday night, if they're feeling tired and mellow.

'That's typical!' I said. 'You tell me off, even though it wasn't my fault, and I wouldn't have dropped it at all if it hadn't been for Joe and Tiffany being horrible!'

'Yes, but if you'd been in the kitchen, love, it would have dropped on to the tiles and it could have been cleared up right away, no problem,' said Mum. 'Now I've got to go and get out the carpet shampoo.'

'I did my best!' I shouted. 'I scrubbed it all off the best I could! And anyway, if I had been having my snack in the kitchen and they'd looked through the window at me that would still have been horrible of them! You don't care about that! You don't care about how frightened I was! All you care about is the blinking carpet!'

'I do care about you, love,' said Mum, looking tired. 'I'm shattered. I've had an awful day. Now I'm going downstairs to make a cup of tea and I'm going to tell Joe what I think of him. I'll put a pizza in the oven for you, OK? And some oven chips. It'll be about twenty minutes. I'll give you a call.'

'I'm not coming down until Tiffany's gone!' I snapped. 'I hate her!'

Mum just sighed and closed the door. I suddenly realised, with a sickening feeling, that the revenge

I'd planned for Joe – putting my pudding in his bed – wasn't really going to bother him all that much. It was just going to be another irritating thing for Mum to have to deal with. And in her present mood, I was certainly going to get shouted at, big time.

I grabbed my phone and texted Holly. *JOE & TFNY PLYD HORRD TRICK ON ME. SCARED ME TO DTH. GOT TO THNK OF RVNGE ON HIM. HELP! LV, RUBY*

A few minutes later a text came back. *LEAVE ME OUT OF IT! THOUGH I WILL, OF COURSE, BE DELIGHTED TO REMAIN YOUR STYLE ADVISER. HOL X*

Silly me. Holly would never want to get involved in a revenge on Joe because she probably secretly still liked him. I was on my own.

Tiffany stayed to supper and ate loads of chips, so we all had to have less. She's always hanging around these days. She and Joe were trading silly jokes.

'Giant Pizza Lands on Kansas,' said Tiffany, snorting with laughter.

'"Aliens Must Be Italian," says Mayor of Kansas City,' added Joe. I get fed up of him talking in headlines, but I hated the way Tiffany was copying it.

After supper I showed my disgust by going upstairs and having a bath. Then I read for a bit, and then I went to bed. I'd just switched my light off when Joe burst into my room, climbed up my ladder and smeared a handful of banana and yogurt all over my face. He'd obviously found his pud-in-a-bed.

Then he laughed an evil laugh and was gone. It was like war, at the moment, between Joe and me.

CHAPTER 5

Stop being so stressy!

NEXT DAY IT was raining. School always seems crowded and noisy on rainy days. Froggo handed me an envelope. Inside was a card decorated with skeletons. *HALLOWE'EN SUPPER AT FROGGO'S with TRICK OR TREATING*, it said in kind of creepy writing.

'Saturday night,' said Froggo. 'Be there or else. I'm going to be a monk with no face, like those Wraith things in *The Lord of the Rings.*'

'Ace,' I said. 'Thanks. I'll be a vampire.'

At break we were in a corner of the classroom

because it was raining outside. Froggo and me, Yasmin and Max. We talked about Hallowe'en for a bit, and Max, who likes making noises, imitated the sound of a vampire getting out of its coffin.

Yasmin was eating her break-time treat – a kind of syrupy cake thing.

'Ruby – wanna taste of my tishpishti?' asked Yasmin.

'Your *what?!?!?!*' said Froggo, rolling his eyes. 'Sounds disguuuuursting!'

Secretly, I think Yasmin's cake *is* a little bit disgusting. It's too sweet for me. And your fingers get covered with goo. I don't think I've got much of a sweet tooth, actually. I think I've got more of a savoury tooth.

'Thanks, Yas,' I said, 'but not today. I'm on a no-sugar diet at the mo – for my teeth, which are basically crumbling away. Now, guys, I need your ideas . . .' I was desperate to think of a trick I could play on Joe in revenge for all the horrible things he'd done to me recently. I'd even been told off this morning because of him. Mum had got quite cross about the pud-in-a-bed episode.

'My teeth are fine,' said Froggo. 'I'll have some cake!'

'I didn't offer any to you,' said Yasmin. 'This is special girls' cake!'

'I don't care,' said Froggo. 'I'm a special girl.'

'Sharks grow new teeth all the time,' said Max. 'This is the sound of a shark eating a shoal of little fishes. *Sssssshhhhh-nark! Sclatter-sclitter! Squeakety squeakety squeeeeeeeee . . .*' It faded out rather sadly.

'Thanks for that, Max,' I said. 'That's ruined my morning. Anyway, I need your ideas –'

'My little sister's tooth came out last night,' said Froggo, 'in a piece of bread and butter. She screamed. But the tooth fairy came in the night and left her £1.'

'Cheapskate,' said Yasmin. 'I used to get £5.'

'Guys, guys, I need your ideas . . .' I said.

'I can't stand these goody-goody fairies,' said Yasmin, finishing her cake and starting to lick her fingers. 'I prefer the bad fairies who come in the night and paint skid marks in everybody's clean pants.'

Froggo and Max laughed. I smiled a bit, but I knew Yasmin hadn't made that joke up herself. She'd got it off Holly last week. I'd been there when Holly and Yasmin's big sister Zerrin were having tea in Yasmin's posh kitchen, talking about alternative Gothic-type fairies.

'Listen!' I shouted. 'I need your ideas, OK! Stop talking about teeth and fairies and stuff and give me some serious suggestions!'

'Suggestions for what?' asked Yasmin, sucking each finger in turn with horrible smacking and slurping noises.

'It's my horrible brother, Joe,' I said. 'He keeps playing tricks on me and I need revenge. But what?'

'This,' said Max, 'is the sound of Joe being attacked by a herd of mad wild horses!' And he went off on a ridiculous whinnying and yelling number. He made such a row, nobody else could say anything until he'd got bored with it. Which was a long time *after* I'd got bored with it, of course.

'Yeah, right,' I said. 'Where am I going to get a herd of wild horses?'

'If you put sugar in the petrol tank of a car,' said Froggo, 'it won't go.'

'Joe hasn't got a car,' I said crossly. I wasn't impressed with any of the ideas so far.

'If I want to play a trick on Zerrin,' said Yasmin, 'I hide her clothes.'

'That wouldn't bother Joe,' I said. 'He'd just go on wearing the same dirty old clothes for days and days. He does that anyway.'

'He's a legend,' said Froggo.

'He is so *not* a legend!' I snapped. 'He's just totally infuriating and I sooo have to think of a revenge! Come *on*!'

'Fill his trainers with frogspawn,' suggested Max, then made the sound of somebody walking around with squelchy frogspawn footsteps.

'It's autumn, dumbo!' I said. 'Nearly winter! There won't be any frogspawn around till next spring. I need revenge and I need it now!'

'Bake him a cake with poison in it,' said Yasmin.

'*Yasmin*!' I was really fed up now. My friends

were totally useless. 'You know I can't cook, for a start. And where would I find some poison? Get real! This isn't a fairy tale!'

'At least I'm trying!' snapped Yasmin. 'Don't yell at me! You asked for ideas, we're giving you some! Stop being so stressy!'

Whoops! I could tell Yasmin was revving up for a row. She sort of likes them. She's a bit of a drama queen. Right now, her eyes flashed and she was waiting for me to snap right back. But I wouldn't.

'Right, that's enough ideas,' I said. 'I'm going to the loo now.' And I strolled off. I hoped I was looking cool, even though I was kind of furious inside.

I went into the girls' loos. I have no choice, really. If only there were three sorts of loos: girls, boys, and gangsters. I had a pee, then washed my hands for ages. Not because I wanted brownie points from God for being hygienic, but because I was thinking. I *had* to come up with a revenge on Joe.

Maybe Froggo's Hallowe'en night would provide a few ideas. I'd already decided to go as a vampire. It could be the start of a major brilliant revenge. I would have to ask Mum to get some more tomato ketchup . . .

CHAPTER 6
Let me go, you loser!

WHEN I GOT home that afternoon, it had rained so much all day, there was a sort of cold mist everywhere. I prayed that Mum or Dad would be home already. But they weren't. And where was Joe? As I unlocked the front door, I couldn't decide if I wanted him to be home or not.

Obviously, if he was home, just sitting watching TV or something, it would make the house seem normal, not so frightening. But if he was hidden away somewhere, waiting to pounce or loom or grab, it made everything a hundred times more scary. I stepped inside and switched on the light.

It seemed OK. I did my special 'I'm home' call, which is rather like a monkey calling from the depths of the forest: *oo-oo-oo-ooo-aah-aah-aah*! If Dad's at home, he makes a monkey noise back, and if Mum's at home, she shouts, 'Hello, love!' from the kitchen. I listened. There was no sound.

I ran around the downstairs, flicking on all the lights and drawing the curtains so nobody could press their faces against the glass. I switched on the TV and turned to *The Simpsons*. Then I went to the kitchen.

I fancied a toasted sandwich. I got two slices of bread and a slice of cheese and assembled them in the sandwich maker. While it was toasting I poured myself a glass of orange juice. I knew that after last time I'd better have my snack in the kitchen, so I made a space on the table, pushing the junk mail and other random stuff out of the way. Our kitchen is never tidy like Yasmin's.

Then my phone rang. It made me jump slightly, but only because the noise was rather sudden. I wasn't expecting it. And I'd changed the ringtone yesterday to a noisy salsa band. I grabbed it. Somebody had left a message on

voicemail. I listened. Maybe Yasmin had had a brilliant idea for a revenge on Joe.

'*Ruby . . . Rogers . . .*' said a deep, growly, sinister sort of voice. '*We've got your monkeys. If you ever want to see them again, follow our instructions . . .*' Then there was a click and the line went dead.

I was so freaked out, I dropped my phone. It bounced on the tiles and the back came off it. But I didn't have time for that now. I raced upstairs, burst into my bedroom and hurled myself up my stepladder into my tree house. The monkeys were all gone!

I burst into tears. I wasn't scared, really. I mean,

it had to be Joe. Who else could have got into the house and taken the monkeys? Normal burglars would have stolen the TV or Dad's laptop or something. Or Mum's old Welsh plates off the dresser.

Of course it was Joe. Another of his nasty, sickening tricks. It had even sounded slightly like him on the phone message. But seeing my tree house without the monkeys was a real shock. It was horrible. It was as if they'd died or something. Which is silly, of course, because toys can't die. But you know what I mean.

The tree house looked bare and ghastly without them. I didn't want to stay here. My toasted cheese sandwich was ready, sending lovely delicious wafts upstairs, but I wasn't hungry any more. I was shaking with rage. What had he done with my monkeys?

Joe's bedroom was the obvious place to look. I hesitated. What if he was in there? I'm always a bit wary of going into his room. It has bad memories. I'd got in a furious temper with him once, gone into his room and smashed one of his sculpture thingies.

He makes things out of wood. They're modern and weird and people think they're wonderful, and when he had an exhibition once there was a big piece about it in the paper and I felt really proud.

Now he's making things in bottles: ships in bottles, messages in bottles. There are a few on his desk. But I knew I could never damage any of them, no matter how furious I was with him. When I did it before, I felt as if I'd been cruel to his pet, or something. Weird. Anyway, I wasn't going to touch anything. I was just going to go in and look for my monkeys.

I knocked on his door. (Ironical, considering what he'd done to me recently. I'm *so* polite and he's such a brute!) There was no reply, no sound. I knocked again, a bit louder. Still silence.

Carefully, I opened the door. The room was obviously empty and quite dark. I switched on the light and looked around. There was the usual mess of clothes and shoes and stuff. Plus an overpowering smell of his aftershave: Stag. Well, I suppose it beats smelly socks.

Joe's not been quite so gross since he started going out with Tiffany. He actually has baths and wears clean socks when he's going out with her. And he powders his feet. And sloshes on the aftershave. The whole room reeked of it.

The most obvious place for him to have hidden the monkeys would be in his wardrobe, of course. And after his horrid trick when he'd hidden in my wardrobe I knew I had to rule the wardrobe out right away. He might be hiding in there even now.

I braced myself so that if he was in there, even dressed as a monster, even if his face was covered in ketchup and he shouted 'WAAAAAAH!' in my face, I wouldn't blink an eyelid. I opened the wardrobe very gradually and gently, my heart beating quite fast even though I knew that if there was anything scary in there, it was only Joe.

There were no monkeys in the wardrobe, and no Joe. Only some of Joe's posh clothes hanging at one end. The rest of the space was taken up with his wooden sculptures all piled up one on top of another.

I sighed and closed the wardrobe door again. Then, suddenly, over on Joe's bed, I noticed an envelope propped up against the wall. It was addressed to me! *Ruby Rogers*, it said. My heart gave a little skip.

I was still nervous, but I began to feel this was quite fun in a way – like a treasure hunt. Maybe the next clue was in the envelope.

I went over to the bed and leant across it to pick

up the envelope. And then, in a split second, it happened. Something *grabbed my ankles*! Something under the bed grabbed both my ankles! I screamed blue murder.

It was Joe, of course – bound to be. Obviously. But still, if you think you're in an empty room and suddenly your ankles are grabbed by somebody or something hiding under the bed, you scream.

'Hah-ah-hah-hah-hah-hah-hah-hah!' came a horrible ape-like call from under the bed.

'Let me go, you loser!' I yelled. 'Give me my monkeys!' I scrabbled and scratched at Joe's fingers and tried to get free. If only I had long talons like Yasmin's sister Zerrin, instead of stumpy little fingernails, useless in a crisis.

My only hope really was to bite – but it's quite hard to bite somebody's hands if they're round your ankles. It's kind of far away.

'Let me go or I'll tell everyone you're scared of the dentist!' I shouted, punching his hands feebly with my puny fists. Just then, rescue arrived. We heard the front door slam. Joe let go.

'Hi, honeys, I'm home!' It was Dad. 'Who's making the toasted cheese sandwiches? I want one!'

I raced out on to the landing. Dad was hanging his coat on the hook behind the front door.

'Dad!' I yelled. 'Joe's played a horrible trick on me! He's stolen my monkeys and he hid under his bed and when I went in there he grabbed my ankles!' Dad looked up for me for a split second and then winked. He hates handing out punishments and sorting out rows. He leaves that sort of thing to Mum.

'Never mind, lovely one,' he said. 'Superman's home. Come down and give me a hug!'

I went down and hugged him and felt safe and nice. But even in the depths of the hug I knew I was going to have to deal with Joe once and for all. I could have forgiven the wardrobe trick, I could (eventually) have forgotten the faces up against the window, but no way was he going to get away with stealing my monkeys and grabbing my ankles like that. I was going to get even. My revenge would have to be devastating. I just hoped there was a website: www.devastatingrevenges.com.

We went into the kitchen. My phone was still in pieces on the floor. Dad picked it up and reassembled it. Then he handed it back.

'See if it works,' he said. 'Send someone a nuisance text.' Then he put the kettle on and started unloading the dishwasher. I had a sudden idea. I texted Holly: *JOE'S STLEN MY MNKYS AND HDDN THM. HOW'S YR EVNG?*

Moments later the answer whizzed back: *MY EVENING OK, THANKS. IGNORE THE IDIOT. DON'T EVEN MENTION THE MONKEYS.* I could see right away this was good advice. Instead of getting angry and creating a scene, I would just be calm and amazing.

Calmly and amazingly, I switched off my mobile and helped Dad lay the table and make a salad. Joe slouched in, looking like a gorilla with a headache.

'Oh yes,' said Dad. 'What was it you'd done? Something to do with Ruby's monkeys?' Joe shrugged. Dad looked at me.

'Oh, forget it,' I said calmly and amazingly. 'I already have.'

Joe looked kind of disappointed that I wasn't in a major strop. I carried my toasted cheese sandwich over to the table and started to eat it. It was cold.

'My sandwich is cold!' I complained. I know I'd planned to be calm and amazing and ignore all the irritating stuff, but there are limits.

CHAPTER 7
We're going to humiliate him

MUM ARRIVED HOME soon afterwards and we all sat down in the kitchen to what she calls an 'improvised supper'. I think that means we make it up as we go along. It ended up with a pudding made from a tin of pears, blackcurrant yogurt and crumbled-up chocolate biscuits. You can't get more improvised than that.

'Right,' said Mum, 'while we're all still here, let's go through the calendar for the next few days.' She fetched the calendar from the wall next to the fridge. 'Hmmm . . . Hallowe'en on Saturday.

We're going to that dinner dance, don't forget, Brian.'

Dad looked startled. 'Two dinner dances in one year?' he said. 'This is cruelty.'

'Shut up!' said Mum with a bouncy grin. 'You're going. It's in aid of the new scanner.'

'Can't I just give them a fiver?' he complained.

'No, you cannot. And don't forget you've got your Parents' Evening the day before – Friday 30th.' Dad went pale and slapped his head.

'My God!' he said. 'I'd totally forgotten!'

'I'd better take your "trustworthy suit" to the cleaners,' said Mum. Dad has a special brown tweed suit which is supposed to make him look like a dependable and sane old geography teacher. It doesn't really work. But he always wears it for Parents' Evenings.

'I assume you'll be out on Friday and Saturday night as usual, Joe?' said Mum. Joe shrugged.

'Whatever,' he said.

'Right! I'll take that's as a yes,' said Mum, writing *JOE OUT* on the calendar.

'It's like being on probation,' grumbled Joe. 'I might as well be tagged or something. Parents Tie Teen to Bedstead for Six Years. "We Just Did It While We Were at a Dinner Dance, at First,' Says

53

Mrs Rogers, 39, of 116 Fairview Road. "But Then It Seemed Like a Good Idea for Every Day, Too."'

'Stop it, Joe!' said Mum, laughing. 'And by the way I'm not thirty-nine! I'm thirty-eight and a half. There *is* a reason why we have to know whether you're going to be out or not.'

'Tell me: I can hardly wait,' said Joe, yawning rudely.

'Well, if we're *all* going to be out, I have to get a babysitter for Ruby.'

'You could just leave her to be eaten by wolves,' said Joe. 'It would solve a lot of problems.'

'You don't have to get a babysitter for me,' I said. 'I get my own.'

'Holly, is it, love? Well, that's fine, then. You'll need one Friday and Saturday, though. I've got to work the evening shift on Friday and Dad's got his Parents' Evening. And then on Saturday there's the dinner dance.'

'Wait!' I had suddenly remembered something. 'I've been invited to a Hallowe'en party on Saturday night, and it's a sleepover.' I ran to my school bag and found Froggo's invitation screwed up in the bottom.

'Oh, right. Well, that's OK for Saturday, then,' said Mum, smoothing out the paper and admiring

Froggo's drawing of skeletons, etc. 'So you just need a babysitter for Friday, Ruby. Ring Holly now, love. Don't leave it till the last minute.'

'OK,' I said, and grabbed my phone. Dad got up and started loading the dishwasher.

'Don't say this meeting is over,' said Joe in a sarcastic voice. 'I was enjoying it *so* much.'

'Don't you go skulking off now!' cried Mum, as he got up. 'Help Dad with the chores!'

'I'll do them tomorrow!' said Joe, and escaped upstairs. Mum sighed, Dad shrugged.

I texted Holly: *CN U BBYSIT ME ON FRI NIGHT? MY VILE BRO REFUSES TO AS HE WILL BE 'OUT'.* This was a subtle way of letting her know that she wouldn't have to face Joe. I had the feeling she was never going to come in and have tea with me after school or babysit for me as long as she had this thing about Joe. She was avoiding him.

She must really have got it bad if she didn't want to see him. I know it must have been a horrid shock for her when he and Tiffany got together, but I would have thought she could follow her own advice and ignore him. Right away a text whizzed back:

SORRY RUBE, I HAVE TO BE OUT FRIDAY

AND SAT. HLLOWE'N YEAH? I'LL FIND U A LOVELY BBYSTTR THOUGH. WATCH THIS SPACE.

I decided to go to my room to try and work out what to wear to Froggo's Hallowe'en party. On the way upstairs, something caught my eye. It was Funky monkey, hanging by his tail from the banisters. I unhooked him and calmly strolled into my room. I wasn't going to make a big thing of it now. My monkeys were going to 'miraculously' reappear.

It had been a horrid shock, though – and the grabbing of the ankles was the last straw. My

revenge – when I thought of it – was going to be ace. I would really make Joe suffer.

I got out my dressing-up box from the bottom of the wardrobe. I usually wear Dad's old black college gown when I'm being a vampire. I couldn't find my plastic fangs, though. To be honest, I was a bit bored with being a vampire. Everybody else would be bound to go as one too.

I went to the loo, hoping for inspiration. As I opened the door, something made me jump for a split second. Stinker, my chief monkey, was sitting on the lavatory – on my old toddler's training seat (which, incidentally, I haven't used for years and years. And *years*).

'At last,' grumbled Stinker. 'What kept yah? A guy doesn't wanna be left like dis. It's kinda humiliating.'

'Don't worry, Stinker,' I promised. '*We're* going to humiliate *him*.'

When I got back to my bedroom, my phone buzzed. I grabbed it. Another text from Holly:

YOUR BBYSTTER FOR FRI IS JESS JORDAN. SHE'S A LUNATIC. YOU'LL LIKE HER. HER NO IS 07789 6799901 – TXT HER DRCT TO LET HER KNO WHT TIME TO ARRV, OK? LV, HOL X

I had a feeling I'd heard Jess's name before
somewhere. I entered her number in my phone's
memory and went down to ask Mum what time
she should come.

Mum was wiping down the table. 'Take your
monkey upstairs, Ruby,' she said. Hewitt was in
the fruit bowl, attacking a banana. 'I don't like toys
in the kitchen,' Mum went on. 'It's unhygienic.'

'But . . .' I was on the verge of saying it wasn't my
fault, it was Joe's, and going off into the whole
story about him grabbing my ankles from under
his bed, and all that stuff, but I decided instead
just to say nothing and be calm and amazing. In a
funny kind of way, it made me feel secretly pow-
erful and strange. I liked it.

CHAPTER 8
I am a complete
and utter idiot

'HI! I'M JESS JORDAN!
Right away I knew where I'd seen her
before. We'd been to one of Joe's school shows last
year, because he'd designed the posters, and Jess
had been in one of the comedy sketches.

It was based on the idea that she had been a tiger
in a previous life, and her flatmate had been a
gazelle, and they had been arguing about whose
turn it was to cook the dinner. The Jess tiger got
annoyed because the gazelle girl was a vegetarian,

and it ended up with the Jess tiger character eating the gazelle girl. It sounds weird but it was really funny.

'Come in!' I said.

Jess hopped inside and then sort of unexpectedly stood still. I bumped into her as I closed the front door.

'Ouch! Sorry!' I said.

'No! My fault!' said Jess.

I felt a bit embarrassed and nervous. It's always strange when you have a new babysitter, and when it's somebody you've seen on stage it's even worse. 'Go through to the kitchen,' I said. 'Mum's in there.'

Jess went through and Mum introduced herself and Dad (who was having a last-minute snack from the fruit bowl).

'We'd better go,' said Mum. 'Anyway . . . thanks so much for agreeing to babysit at such short notice.'

'It's a pleasure,' said Jess. 'I've heard a lot about Ruby. She's a walking legend.' She gave me a beaming smile. I felt slightly shocked, to be honest. A walking legend! However was I going to live up to *that*?

'Right,' said Mum. 'We must be off. Here's our

phone number in case of emergency. And I've left you a little snack.'

'Fantastic!' said Jess. 'I've already eaten a pie the size of a planet this evening, but hey! I like a challenge.'

She did look a little bit chubby from behind, actually. She was way less stylish than Holly, and not so tall.

Mum and Dad went off, and Jess and I kind of stood around awkwardly in the kitchen. On the table Mum had left a couple of dishes covered in cling film. One was a salad and one was a lasagne. Mum had left a note which read: *Switch on oven to 200. Wait five mins. Put lasagne in oven. After twenty-five mins, it should be sizzling, so take it out.*

'Wow! Lasagne! My favourite!' said Jess. 'Let's heat it up! I won't be able to eat a huge amount, though. I'm already bloated from that pie. I feel like one of those puffer fish.' She switched on the oven.

I didn't know what to say. I felt horribly shy. Jess wasn't as pretty as Holly but she did have wild-looking eyebrows and sparkly eyes. Her hair was short and dark and a bit messy, but her smile was huge, and when she smiled she had a tiny dimple on her left cheek.

'So you're the sister of the famous Joe Rogers?' said Jess. 'You don't look a bit like him.'

'Phew!' I said, trying to be amusing, since Jess was apparently into comedy. However, just as I said *phew* the fridge gave one of its regular sighs, and I don't think she heard me. I felt so self-conscious. I couldn't think of anything to say. Jess would assume I was a total nerd.

'Would you like a drink?' I asked.

'Too right!' grinned Jess. 'I thought you'd never ask. Make it a whisky and soda and keep 'em coming.' She said this in a kind of cowboy voice.

For a split second I was stunned. Did she really want a proper grown-up drink? I knew we did have some whisky in the cupboard in the sitting room, because Dad has a glass of whisky and lemon whenever he's got a sore throat. But surely she shouldn't touch it? Wasn't it actually illegal for people under eighteen?

'C'mon, bartender!' said Jess in an American film voice. 'Gimme a Jack Daniels and go easy on the ice!' I felt myself blush, which was really stupid.

'I don't think we're really allowed to have proper drinks, I mean − like − er . . .' I felt the same as in the *Aladdin* rehearsal: my mind had gone totally

blank. I had forgotten the word for proper drinks. 'Ac – ac – accolol, er – whisky.'

Jess threw back her head and laughed and laughed. I stood there, feeling like an idiot. 'Sorry, Ruby,' she said. 'That was a joke. I'm always kidding around. Juice will be fine.'

I got some juice from the fridge and poured it out, but my hand was shaking. I felt like a complete and utter idiot. She had totally made a fool of me. She hadn't meant to, but anyway . . . whatever.

'I've just got to go upstairs for a minute,' I said. 'Excuse me.' I ran upstairs and locked myself in the bathroom. It reeked of Joe's aftershave. He'd been in there half an hour ago, getting ready to go out with Tiffany. I wished I was a teenager. It sucks, sometimes, being a kid.

I sat down on the loo even though I didn't want a pee. Well, where else are you going to sit in the bathroom? I felt so ashamed that I hadn't realised Jess was joking. She must think I was a total idiot. It was nice and private in the bathroom. I was tempted to stay there for the whole evening.

Eventually the delicious smell of lasagne began to creep up the stairs. It overcame the smell of Joe's aftershave and circled round me, making my tummy rumble. I washed my hands and went downstairs.

'Are you OK?' Jess looked anxious. She had laid two places at the kitchen table.

'Oh yeah,' I said. *Yeah* sounded cooler than *yes*. 'I just read a bit of my book. You know. I got well into it and I didn't realise what time it was.'

Jess looked relieved. 'Fantastic!' She said. 'I love reading. What book is it?'

My mind went blank again. I panicked. I couldn't think of a single book, even though I have my own bookcase in my bedroom and it's absolutely packed with books. My heart raced. I felt hot. I

knew I was blushing. I couldn't think of a single book title in the whole wide world.

'*My Life as a Gangster* by Stinker Apeworth,' I said in desperation, inventing a title. Jess looked interested – too interested.

'I've never heard of that,' she said. 'I'd like to look at it later. Is it a children's book or a book for adults?'

'Er, neither,' I said, and sat down at the table. 'I mean, both. Is the lasagne ready?'

Jess got the lasagne out and we ate supper. Once again I was totally unable to think of a single thing to say. Jess was so cool – she was the comedy queen of Ashcroft School – and yet I couldn't talk to her. I ate a bit of lasagne miserably.

Jess talked a lot, in a gabbly sort of way, about random things. How much she liked our curtains. How much she loved our table. Her own kitchen table was way inferior, apparently. How great our floor tiles were. I was just speechless. It was as if my brain had turned into a doughnut.

'OK,' said Jess, after supper. 'What next? A movie? A game of snakes and ladders? You name it, I'm up for it. Let's take a look at your collection of DVDs.'

'I'm sorry,' I said. 'But I feel really tired. I think I should go to bed.' I wanted to stay but I just had to escape. I was being so lame, it was ridiculous. Jess looked surprised.

'Really?' she said. 'Oh, I forgot, you're just a kid. Kids go to bed early, don't they? What a shame. Never mind. Just show me where your DVDs are and I'll wallow in them all by myself.'

I took her into the sitting room, showed her how to work everything, and then hesitated. I *so* wanted to apologise for my stupid shyness and thank her for putting up with me. And tell her I wasn't always so boring. But instead I just said, 'Good night then, Jess.'

'Good night, Ruby!' said Jess, grinning with the dimple again. 'Great to meet you.'

Suddenly I was scared she might try and kiss me good night, so I ran off upstairs to my room. It looked as if I was condemned to a long evening playing with my monkeys in a lonesome way, while the most amusing girl in the world watched movies without me downstairs. It was only eight o'clock, for goodness' sake. It seemed later because it was so dark outside.

'Monkeys,' I announced sadly. 'I am a complete and utter idiot.'

'We've always thought so,' said Funky sadly. 'But we were too kind to mention it.'

CHAPTER 9

What the hell was that?

THE MONKEYS DIDN'T seem to be in the mood for fun. Stinker was trying to take a nap. 'Quit messin' wid me!' he growled. 'Can't a guy get a bit of shut-eye round here?'

Funky had tied himself in a mean knot and was staring at me from just above his bottom. 'I've got problems,' he said. 'I've got to get in touch with my inner monkey and face my demons. And I've got to do it alone.'

'What about you, Hewitt?' I asked. 'How about a game of tennis?'

Hewitt sighed. 'Not tonight, babe,' he said. 'I've got a headache.'

'OK,' I said, and reached for one of my favourite books. I was halfway into chapter three, where a vegetarian vampire called Vincent finds a wonderful fruit called a blood orange, when suddenly, *WHOOP*! All the lights went out.

All the machines in the house sort of died too. Everything was black and silent. Instantly I got goosebumps. What had happened? Had an intruder fiddled with the electricity so he could burgle us in comfort? My wardrobe creaked.

Isn't that just like a wardrobe? It knows you're a tiny bit scared of it, it remembers the time your brother hid in there with his fleece pulled over his head to make him look like a monster, but does it creak in daylight, or when the light's on? Of course not. It creaks when you're suddenly plunged into the dark, of course.

I scrambled down my ladder. Jess was downstairs. She would defend me from intruders and protect me from creaking wardrobes. It was her job, right? I tiptoed to the door and opened it. It creaked eerily: *eeeeeeee-aaaaaaaah*!

Out on the landing, my eyes began to get used to the dark. Thank goodness Joe was really out this time. I'd actually *seen* him leave. I crept downstairs and edged my way into the sitting room. I couldn't see much in there. The curtains were thick and it was almost total blackout.

'Jess?' I whispered. 'Jess?' There was no reply. My hair nearly stood on end. Oh lordy! She *wasn't there*!

I inched my way through the room, my eyes gradually getting used even to this deep darkness. There was nobody on the sofa. Nobody on the chairs. Nobody. I touched the seat of the sofa. It was warm. So moments ago she'd been here.

My babysitter had been abducted by aliens! Or possibly kidnapped very quietly by a man wearing black velvet gloves and rubber-soled shoes. My heart gave a horrid sickening lurch. I tiptoed back out into the hall. And then I heard it. In the cupboard under the stairs. *Rustling.*

Was it a ghost? Was it a rat? Was it an alien wearing rubber gloves and a velvet hat? I tiptoed nearer. Right up to the door. I bent down a bit. The door was open a crack. I listened. There was definitely rustling.

Suddenly the door opened and hit me on the side of the head. I yelled in pain, stumbled sideways and fell on the floor.

'Oh my God!' I heard a voice say. It sounded familiar. 'Is it you, Ruby? I'm so sorry!'

'I'm sorry,' I said, getting up, rubbing my head and feeling like an idiot again. 'I heard a noise . . . but it was only you. I'm OK . . . fine.'

'I heard a noise too!' said Jess, crawling out of the cupboard like a kitten out of a cardboard box. 'I heard a noise upstairs – but it must have been you.'

'What were you doing under the stairs?' I asked.

'I just wanted to check . . . to see if a fuse had blown,' said Jess.

'Oh. And has it?' There was a pause.

'No. Er . . . I'm going to be honest with you, Ruby. I was hiding under there because I was scared absolutely *witless*!' And Jess started to giggle, and rolled about on the floor in the dark. I started to giggle too. A babysitter who was more scared of the dark than I was!

'OOOOH, crikey,' groaned Jess, coming to the end of her laugh. 'Oooooh, Lordy. That was so funny. Oh dear. I am sorry, Ruby. I am *insane*. I take it I'm fired?'

'Oh, no!' I said. 'I quite like having a scaredy babysitter. It makes me feel not so scared myself.'

Just then there was a horrible noise in the sitting

room: *SCHNAK!* Jess grabbed me and cowered down on to my shoulder.

'What the hell was that?' she whispered. 'It sounded like an intruder sharpening his whatyamacallit!'

'It's just the noise the telly makes when it's cooling down,' I said.

'Phew!' said Jess. 'Sorry, I'm a bag of nerves.'

'An intruder sharpening his whatyamacallit wouldn't sound like that,' I said. 'It would go more like this: *SREEEEECH SREEECH SREEEEEEEECH!*'

'You're so right!' agreed Jess. 'Hey! I've just had an idea for a brilliant game. You go into the sitting room, and I'll stay out here, and we'll make scary noises at each other.'

'Great idea!' I said. This evening was starting to be fun after all. 'Only one thing. You're going to be the one going into the sitting room.'

'Just in case that sound *wasn't* the telly cooling down after all, you mean?' whispered Jess. 'OK. I'm boldly going . . . See you later . . . Whose go is it first?'

'Yours,' I said. Jess tiptoed back into the sitting room, and then suddenly gave a blood-curdling shriek. My heart leapt.

'Are you OK?' I called. Then I heard Jess giggling helplessly, like a panting dog.

'First score to me!' she shouted. 'Fifteen love!' This was more fun than ordinary tennis.

I waited until it was quiet again. Then I started breathing. I crept up to the sitting-room door and breathed like a very heavy monster with rolls of fat round its neck. '*MMMMMMM-aaaaaaaah! MMMMMMM-aaaaaaah! MMMMMMM—*' Then I inhaled a bit of spit and had a coughing fit. Then we both got the giggles again: Jess in the sitting room, me out in the hall.

'The breathing was brilliant, though,' said Jess. 'It totally made me wet myself with fear. Mentally, I mean, not for real. Fifteen all. My turn now.'

There was a brief pause. I waited out in the hall. Then suddenly, *WHGOOOOP*! All the lights came on and all the machines started up and the TV started to blare and jabber, all at once, in an explosion of brightness and noise.

'Help!' yelled Jess. 'That was the scariest thing so far! How did you do it, Ruby?' she came out into the hall, screwing her eyes up in the light.

'That was a great game,' I said. 'It's really annoying that the lights have come on again.'

'We could go on playing it if we switch the lights off,' said Jess. 'Or would you rather share a cup of hot chocolate and tell me all your problems?'

'Hot choc!' I grinned, and we surfed off to the kitchen.

'I only have two problems,' I said, as Jess put the kettle on. 'But they are *major*.'

'I'll sort it out for you. Tell Auntie Jess. If I don't come up with a brilliant solution, you're welcome to cover me with fried onions and ketchup and call me Hot Dog of the Year.'

CHAPTER 10
It's too wicked for words!

'WELL, MY FIRST problem is, I have stage fright,' I said. 'I'm in the school play – *Aladdin*. I've only got a small part, but I get so scared, even at rehearsals. I kind of seize up and forget my lines.'

'Don't worry!' grinned Jess. 'Just make something up. Chances are it'll be better than the real lines.'

'When I said "Happy Pancake" instead of "Hanky Panky", everybody thought I was a no-brain and laughed at me.'

'They weren't laughing in a nasty way,' said Jess.

'They were laughing cos you're funny. A natural comedian. People love that sort of thing. If you forget your lines, don't panic. Just exaggerate it. Don't try to cover it up. Act deliberately dumb. Just scratch your head and pull a face and say something completely random. Problem solved?'

'Hmmmm,' I said. It sounded a bit dangerous, but it kind of gave me a lifeline. 'The thing is, when we perform it properly, at the end of term, there'll be loads and loads of people all staring at me. I just *know* I'm going to faint or be sick or fall over or something. All those faces looking at me.'

'But you won't be able to see them at the performance,' said Jess. 'It'll be cool. The lights will go down and the audience will be sitting in the dark.'

I shuddered. 'The dark! That's my worst phobia of all. But the real problem is Joe,' I explained. 'He knows I'm afraid of the dark, and he keeps playing these horrid tricks on me.' I told her about the headless monster in the wardrobe, and the faces pressed up against the window, and the ankle-grabbing thing under the bed.

'What a plonker!' said Jess. 'Getting his kicks from scaring a little girl.'

'I've got to get my revenge,' I said. 'But I can't think of anything.'

'I know,' said Jess. 'Let's go up to his room and have a look around. It might give me an idea.'

We went up to Joe's bedroom. Although I knew he was out, I had to look in his wardrobe and under his bed, just in case. Jess sniffed.

'What's this smell?' she asked.

'It's his aftershave,' I said. 'Ever since he started going out with Tiffany, he pours the stuff all over himself. It's over there, on that shelf.'

Jess went over to the shelf and picked up the dark brown bottle. It said Stag on it, and there was a picture of a deer with enormous antlers silhouetted against the moon. Jess unscrewed the top and examined the bottle. It had a sort of stopper

thing inside so the aftershave came out in little drops.

Jess looked around the room and saw a pair of scissors. She picked them up and levered off the stopper. It came out quite easily. She peeped into the bottle and sloshed it about. It was half full.

Then she looked at me, and it was the naughtiest look I have ever seen. Her eyes were dancing with devilish delight.

'I've had an idea,' she said. 'But I'm afraid it's totally evil.'

'Tell me!' I said.

'It's the most disgusting thought I've ever had,' she went on. 'It's vile.'

'Tell me!!!'

'It's too wicked for words,' said Jess, grinning so widely another dimple appeared on the other side of her face as well.

'*Tell* me!!!!!' I yelled.

'Here's what we do,' said Jess. 'We throw the rest of this away. And then we fill the bottle up with something else.'

'What?' I begged. 'Tell me! – *What?*'

Jess screwed her eyes shut, pursed her mouth up and wrinkled her nose.

'With pee!' she said in a sort of squeak.

'With pee?!' I gasped. I felt sick, I felt disgusted, I felt faint and I felt triumphant. Victory was mine! My pee would be on his neck.

'What a truly sickening idea,' I said. 'Awesome! But how am I ever going to manage to pee into that little bottle?'

Jess thought for a moment or two.

'You'll have to pee in a saucepan or something,' she said. 'Or a milk jug.'

'A milk jug!' I screamed. 'No way!' But somehow, I could already imagine myself doing it. In fact, I think I might have done something similar once, in a dream.

'Then we pour it from the milk jug into the bottle,' said Jess, smiling evilly. 'Come on, Ruby! Let's go and get a jug or something.'

We went downstairs and looked round the kitchen. Peeing into any of the kitchen pots and pans seemed totally vile.

'Don't worry,' said Jess. 'We can wash it seven times afterwards. And scald it in boiling water. And anyway, there's more bacteria in your saliva than there is in your pee. I saw it on a science programme on TV.'

'You're making this up!' I said. I got the feeling now that Jess was going to land me in the most awful trouble. But I didn't care. I felt kind of thrilled to bits. Joe was going to get a revenge worthy of his many crimes.

Jess selected a saucepan and a milk jug and gave me a questioning look. I began to tremble.

'Don't bother with the saucepan,' I said. 'I'll pee straight into the jug. I don't want to pee very much anyway.'

'Come on, then,' said Jess. We went back upstairs. I hoped she wasn't expecting to come into the bathroom with me. That stuff's private.

She did come in, but only to empty Joe's bottle of aftershave down the plughole. The perfume was overpowering. Jess ran cold water and sloshed it round the basin, and gradually the smell cleared. She placed the bottle on the windowsill.

'OK,' she said. 'Now, all you have to do is pee for England. In the jug. I'll pour it in the bottle afterwards.' She handed me the milk jug and went out.

I locked the door and stood and stared at the jug. How was I going to do this? The milk jug was way too small to sit on. Maybe I needed the saucepan after all . . . ? No! That would be worse. I'd have to sit on the loo and sort of hold the milk jug in place when the right moment arrived.

So I sat on the loo and waited. And waited. And

waited. There wasn't the faintest, remotest hint of a pee.

'I can't pee!' I said.

'Drink some water!' called Jess from the landing.

I got up and drank two glasses straight off. I sat on the loo again. Nothing.

'It's not working!' I said. 'I can't!'

'Think of water!' came Jess's voice. 'Waterfalls . . . gushing streams, tremendous torrents, the bath taps running full on . . . Cascading, splashing, streaming, bubbling water!'

That did the trick! I started to pee – I shoved the milk jug in place – I caught some of it – and ended up peeing on my hand. Ugh! Gross!

Never mind. I had managed to catch a bit in the jug. I jumped off the loo, placed the milk jug carefully on the windowsill, pulled the flush and washed my hands.

'Any luck?' called Jess.

'Yeah!' I answered. 'All that water talk did the trick. I didn't get much, though.'

'We don't need much,' said Jess. 'When it comes to slapping stuff on your face, a very little pee will go a long way, I find.' I started to giggle and let her in.

Jess picked up the jug.

'Don't touch it!' I screamed. 'Don't look at my pee! It's private! Don't sniff it!'

'Don't be an idiot, Ruby,' said Jess, expertly pouring the pee into Joe's aftershave bottle. 'Everybody's pee is the same. It's normal. It's just coloured water. Even the Queen pees every day.' This thought was so odd, I couldn't think about anything else for a moment.

By the time I'd come out of a kind of fantasy of loos in the Palace, Jess had finished the job, put the stopper back in, screwed the lid back on the bottle, rinsed it quickly and dried it. She also washed the milk jug – but to be honest, if she'd washed the milk jug seventeen times an hour for the rest of her entire life, it would never have been washed quite *enough*.

We went into Joe's bedroom and placed the bottle back on his shelf where we'd found it. My heart was beating quite fast. A small part of me wanted to turn back the clock and undo this disgusting thing we'd just done.

'Don't get cold feet, Ruby,' said Jess, staring at me sternly. 'He deserves this. He deserves worse than this. Think of how he frightened you.'

'OK,' I said. But I still felt ever so slightly sick. We went downstairs. Jess washed the milk jug again, then scalded it with boiling water, then put it in the dishwasher with all the dirty dishes. We ran the hottest cycle.

'That's it, then,' said Jess. 'Do you fancy a music video before you go to bed?'

I did, but I couldn't really concentrate. And even afterwards, when I was in bed, long after Mum and Dad had come home and Jess had gone, I wasn't properly asleep. I heard Joe come in, really late, and go into his room. Would he put some aftershave on now? It seemed unlikely. Tonight he would just fall into bed. Tomorrow would be the day when he'd unscrew the magic bottle . . .

CHAPTER 11
Brilliant! Great idea!

I WOKE UP NEXT day feeling really grouchy because I'd slept so badly. Joe, of course, lay in bed till lunchtime. This was a bit of a relief. I kept wondering what it would be like when he opened the bottle . . . and sloshed some on to his hand . . . and patted it all round his face . . . UGH!

It ought to have been hilarious, and I think I would have been crazy with excitement if Jess had still been with me. Or even another of my friends to share the secret. I was really nervous, so nervous I almost felt sick.

'Cornflakes, Ruby?' said Mum. The milk jug was on the table. I tried to think of something else.

'No, thanks,' I said. 'Just toast, please, Mum.' She made it, and I ate it, and though it was with my favourite, Marmite, it took ages to eat it. I almost had to force it down.

'You look a bit pale, love,' said Mum. 'I hope you're not sickening for something. You've got that Hallowe'en party tonight as well.'

The party! Froggo's trick-or-treat party! I had totally forgotten about that. I couldn't believe it. I was so pleased. I'd be out from about five o'clock, then. I might miss the moment when Joe unscrewed his bottle and . . . In a funny kind of way, I almost hoped I *would* miss the moment.

'Dad and I have got our dinner dance, too,' said Mum, organising everything in her busy way. 'Right. Brian, you'll have to take Ruby round to Dan's house for five o'clock while I'm in the bath. What are you wearing, Ruby?'

Suddenly I realised my Hallowe'en costume sucked. All I had was Dad's old black college gown. And I'd discovered yesterday that my plastic fangs were broken.

'I don't know,' I said, finishing my juice. 'I think

I'll go and have a look in the dressing-up box. PleasemayIleavethetable?'

Mum nodded. I ran upstairs and got out the dressing-up box. There was nothing that would do for Hallowe'en. Without my fangs I was hopeless. There would be loads of vampire costumes tonight and I didn't want mine to be the worst.

Suddenly I heard Joe get up. He flung his door open – and I actually *cringed*, expecting him to come bursting in and possibly empty the whole contents of the magic bottle over my head! Omigawd! He would so *totally* do that when he found out! Or possibly something even *worse*! This stupid idea of Jess's was *so* the worst thing I had ever done!

I heard Joe go into the bathroom. Thank God. After a couple of minutes he flushed the loo, and returned to his room. Silence fell. He'd gone back to bed. After a minute or two I stopped trembling. Joe had gone to sleep again. I was safe till he got up properly.

If only I had somebody to share this with! I grabbed my phone and rang Yasmin.

'Hi Ruby!' she said.

'Hey, Yas,' I said in my gangster's voice. I didn't want to sound too needy. 'I gotta problem. I wanna talk it froo wid ya.'

'Sorry, Rube!' said Yas. 'I can't talk now. My mum and I are in town getting my Hallowe'en costume sorted out. I've got this brilliant witch's hat with rubber spiders hanging from it. See you tonight! Tell me all about it then! Bye!'

So much for help and support from my best buddy. I sat and thought for a minute. Then I had a great idea. I rang Holly. She picked up almost immediately.

'Hi, Holly!' I said, trying to sound amusing and relaxed, not scared and useless.

'Hey, Ruby!' said Holly. 'How did it go last night? Did you like Jess?'

'Yeah, she was great,' I said. 'A bit crazy, though.'

I was on the point of telling her all about it, when I heard Mum come upstairs and start sorting out some linen in the airing cupboard, which is just outside my bedroom door. I didn't dare mention anything about the magic bottle in case she overheard.

'So, you all set for your Hallowe'en party tonight?' asked Holly.

'Well, I've got a bit of a prob,' I explained. 'I usually go as a vampire but I've broken my fangs, and the costume isn't very good anyway. I was wondering if you could possibly come over and do me a special make-up. A Hallowe'en face. A ghost or something. Sorry to bother you,' I added lamely. There was a horrid pause.

I knew she was thinking about Joe being here, and the possibility that he might ignore her, messing about with Tiffany right under her nose.

'I haven't got a lot of time today, Ruby,' she said. 'I've got to get ready for my own Hallowe'en party, right? I don't have time to do you a face. I'm really sorry.' I felt crushed.

'But I do have a spare cossie. I've been messing around with various costumes and I've got a couple of masks and a cloak . . . If you'd like to go as a sinister little fiery imp?'

'Brilliant!' I said. 'Great idea! I'd love to! Thanks so much!'

'I'll drop it round later, then,' said Holly. 'I'm not quite sure when. OK? Bye!'

Mum opened my bedroom door.

'Ruby!' she said. 'Get off that phone! You know it's only for emergencies!'

'This is an emergency,' I said, switching the phone off. Mum shook her head as if I was the last straw, and placed some clean clothes in a drawer. 'Holly's coming round later to lend me a Hallowe'en outfit,' I told her. 'I'm going to Froggo's party as a fiery imp.'

'Oooh, that's lovely,' said Mum. 'Holly's so original.' And she bustled out. She was dead right. Holly *was* original. If only my useless brother could see it and be Holly's boyfriend instead of wasting his time with the trashy Tiffany.

Mum went into Joe's bedroom and woke him up with a lot of shaking and yelling. Oh no! Now he was going to get up, there was a chance he'd open the magic bottle. I felt sick with fear.

CHAPTER 12
That should do the trick!

THIS WAS RIDICULOUS. I was more scared of Joe opening the bottle than I had been when Joe had played all those frightening tricks on me. It wasn't just fear. It was worse: guilt. Joe had been really horrible to me, and he deserved to be peed on by a whole pack of wild dogs, but I still wished I hadn't asked Jess's advice about how to get revenge on Joe.

On the other hand, Joe *did* deserve it. He'd been vile. I heard him now, slouching to the bathroom and slamming the door. My heart started to beat really fast. Now he was getting up and getting dressed and stuff, he might fancy a splash of after-shave. After all, it was Saturday.

I ran downstairs and into the garden. Dad was painting the fence. I tried to look casual and cool. I went into the greenhouse and pretended to admire the plants in there. At this time of year, though, everything was sort of dying down for the winter. Most of the pot plants had been pruned back and they were just little sticks.

There was a big wide shelf on both sides of the greenhouse, and plenty of room under the shelf to hide. I found a corner under there and sat down. After a while, Dad's face appeared in the doorway.

'What are you doing in there?' he asked. Mum would have told me to get up because I'd dirty my clothes, or she'd be worried about me hurting myself on something, but Dad just grinned. 'Are you a little toad planning to hibernate?'

'I'm playing hide-and-seek,' I said. 'Don't tell anybody where I am.'

'OK,' said Dad, and he winked as if he was joining in some delightful game. If only he knew. He went back to painting his fence, and I sat curled up under the greenhouse staging until my feet went to sleep.

Then I had to crawl out and hobble about on the lawn to get rid of the pins and needles. I wondered if it was safe to go indoors. It was quite chilly outside. I peeped in through the sitting-room window – the one Joe and Tiffany had pressed their faces against. There was nobody in the sitting room.

I had to risk it. I crept in through the back door. Mum was peeling some onions in the kitchen.

'Mum,' I said. 'Where's Joe?'

'He went out, love,' said Mum, sniffing and wiping her eyes. 'Why?'

'I just didn't want to bump into him,' I said, speedily inventing something and probably looking guilty as anything. 'He keeps playing frightening tricks on me and scaring me to death.'

'That's what brothers are for, Ruby,' said Mum, blowing her nose on a piece of kitchen roll. 'Instead of moaning about it, you should play some tricks back on *him!*' She looked at me as though I was an idiot. If only she knew.

I went upstairs to see if there was any sign of Joe having opened the magic bottle. I peeped into his room. The bottle was in exactly the same position as when Jess and I had put it back last night. I got the feeling he hadn't touched it. Joe doesn't usu-

92

ally start sloshing on his aftershave until he goes out in the evening. With any luck, by then I'd be at my party.

The rest of the day was reasonably relaxed, though I was a bit nervous in case Joe came back. The highlight of the afternoon was when Holly dropped by with my costume. The fiery cloak was lovely, made from bits of cloth cut up and stitched together, and the mask was amazing and mysterious with a long cruel nose like a beak.

'I can't stop,' said Holly, once I'd put it on. 'Got to get my own costume sorted.' Mum was in the kitchen with us, admiring Holly's creative gifts, so I couldn't mention the magic bottle.

'What are you going to your party as, Holly?' asked Mum.

'I thought I'd go as a zombie this time,' said Holly. 'It's a major make-up challenge. It's going to take three hours.'

'Take a photo of yourself when you're finished,' I said. 'I'd love to see it.'

'Of course,' said Holly, backing off towards the door. You could see she was worried in case Joe came downstairs. I felt sorry for her. I wanted to tell her not to worry, Joe was out, but that was too obvious. So I just thanked her for the wonderful costume and waved my impish cloak about.

After Holly had gone, Mum suggested I have a quick snack in case there wasn't much tea at Froggo's, or in case we didn't eat till late, or something. She made me a toasted sandwich. Dad came in from the garden.

'I've finished that fence,' he said. 'But I think I've strained my back.'

'You're not getting out of going to this dinner dance, Brian!' said Mum half sternly and half playfully. 'You have a nice long soak in a hot bath and you'll soon feel better. You need one anyway — that wood treatment stuff smells awful!'

Dad went off to have his bath. I went on eating

my sandwich. Mum got the ironing board out and started ironing a clean shirt for Dad. The phone rang. Mum answered it.

'Hello, love!' It was Joe, then. 'Right . . . right . . . right . . . You've got your key, have you? All right then. Have a lovely time, and don't drink too much!' She rang off, and then got on with ironing her dress.

'Was that Joe?' I asked, trying to sound casual.

'Yes. He's not coming back for tea,' said Mum. 'He's out with his mates and he's going straight on to the party at the Town Hall.'

Phew! Huge relief flooded through me. I could relax and enjoy Hallowe'en without worrying about Joe coming home and opening the magic bottle. I realised, at this moment, how deeply I regretted having played this trick. Even though Joe deserved it, it just wasn't worth the hassle. I'd been in agony all night and most of the day.

Dad came downstairs in his dressing gown. He'd washed his hair and he looked shiny and nice.

'Where's my clean shirt?' he asked.

'Here,' said Mum. 'Don't crumple it, mind.' She'd put it on a coat hanger and as she handed it to him, she hesitated. And sniffed.

'Brian, I can still smell that blinking fence paint,'

she said. 'It's only a faint whiff, but it's really off-putting. Go and put a bit of aftershave on, love.'

'My aftershave's finished,' said Dad. 'I finished the last of it when we were on holiday and I haven't had any since. And nobody's given me any.' He put on a doleful, sorry-for-himself expression, hoping to make me laugh. But I couldn't laugh. I was rooted to the spot by all this talk of after-shave. I could see what was coming. It was heading for me just like a runaway big red bus. Disaster was about to strike. My heart was hammering like mad.

'Well, borrow a bit of Joe's, then, love,' said Mum. 'It's on that shelf in his bedroom. Stag, it's called. In a brown bottle. I think it smells lovely. Splash a bit of that round your gills. That should do the trick!'

CHAPTER 13
Let's creep up on them!

'W HERE'S HE KEEP it, then?' asked
Dad. He was fiddling with the radio dial.
'We don't need the news. It's too depressing. Let's
have a samba band!' He found some music.

'I know where it is!' I yelled. 'I'll get it!' My dad
started dancing to the music. I raced upstairs.

I burst into Joe's room, my heart thumping so
hard I almost fainted. There was the bottle, sitting
on its shelf, looking so innocent. I had to get rid of
it now! Any moment Dad might come dancing
upstairs and slosh my pee all over his face!

I opened the window, grabbed the bottle and threw it out into the night. A split second later there was a sudden *CRASH! – Tinkle, tinkle . . .* Oh no! It had smashed clean into the greenhouse!

I closed the window and started to tremble. I trembled so hard I sort of shivered. All the flames on my cloak fluttered. I had broken a pane of glass in the greenhouse! And when my parents found out how, they'd be furious! Pee in a bottle! Why had I got myself into this mess? Why had I listened to Jess Jordan? She'd told me herself she was insane.

'Ruby! Ruby!' My mum was calling up the stairs. Perhaps they'd heard the sound of breaking glass. I cringed. There was nowhere to hide. I wished I was in South America. 'Hurry up!' she called. 'We've got to get you to Dan's by five!'

I went downstairs. My legs were shaking. But my parents were just standing about in the kitchen, talking. The samba music was still on the radio. It was quite loud. So they hadn't heard the bottle smashing into the greenhouse, out in the dark.

'I can't find it,' I said. 'He must have taken it with him.'

'What?' said Mum, looking distracted.

'Joe's aftershave.'

'Oh, never mind that, pet! I can find that while

Dad takes you to Dan's. Are you ready to go? Are you going to be warm enough?'

The bottle of Joe's aftershave hardly seemed to matter to her. If only she knew!

'I've got my gloves,' I said. 'And this cloak is really warm.' I could hardly have a normal conversation, I was so stressed out about the greenhouse. But they didn't notice. Dad drove me to Dan's, and I joined the gang.

'Amazing costume, Ruby!' said Yasmin. 'What's it supposed to be?' She was dressed in a witch's outfit complete with dangling spiders. Dan was The Wraith, with a black face and a dark cloak with a

hood. Max was wearing a skeleton suit. Hannah was, of course, a vampire – and her teeth were really great.

'I'm a fiery imp from the blackest pits of hell,' I said, and pulled down my mask. 'Holly made this costume.'

'Wow!' said Hannah. 'It's amaaaaaazing!'

'Come on, then,' said Froggo. 'We're going to go trick-or-treating for an hour first, and then we're going to have tea.'

We went out and started to work our way down Froggo's road. All his neighbours gave us treats – mostly sweets.

'Maybe we shouldn't eat the sweets now,' said Hannah. 'In case it ruins our appetite for our tea.' She can be such a goody-goody at times.

'Get a life, Hannah!' said Yasmin, smuggling a sherbet lemon past the dangling spiders guarding her face. 'These sherbet lemons are brilliant. They like explode in your mouth. Have one, Ruby.'

I sucked a sweet, but I didn't really want one. I felt almost detached from this trick-or-treat business. I was so worried about what would happen at home when my parents discovered the smashed green-house, and the bottle, and the smell of pee . . .

At the end of Froggo's street is a round bit of road called The Circus. It's nothing to do with clowns or anything, it's just a sort of circle with trees all round it and there are some benches under the trees. It's almost like a bit of a park.

'Look!' hissed Yasmin suddenly, 'There's your bro over there! With Tiffany!' My heart sort of jumped. It was true. Joe and Tiffany were sitting on a bench at the other side of The Circus. They hadn't got their arms round each other and they weren't kissing or anything. They were just sitting there, talking. They hadn't seen us, of course, because it was dark. And even if they did see us, they would- n't recognise us because of our costumes.

'Let's creep up and spook them out!' whispered Yasmin.

'No,' said Froggo. 'That would be stupid. They're not going to give us any treats, are they? Come on, Max, let's do these houses now.'

Dan and Max went up a garden path at our side of The Circus, and Hannah followed them, shrug- ging to us. Yasmin grabbed my arm.

'Come on – just for a min!' she said. 'It'll be fun! Let's creep up on them!' I didn't want to, but I know what Yasmin's like when she gets an idea in her head – she just won't let it go.

'OK, then,' I whispered. We tiptoed round the edge of The Circus, until we were much closer to Joe and Tiffany. They had their backs to us. Then something odd happened. Joe started, well, sort of shouting.

'Fine!' he yelled. 'Great! It's fine!' But he didn't sound as if it was fine. He sounded furious. Then, all of a sudden, he jumped up. We crouched behind a tree.

'Wait! Joe!' said Tiffany. He glared down at her. She mumbled something and sort of feebly held out her hand, to try and hold on to him.

'No!' said Joe. 'No! There's no need to say anything more! I get the picture! I'm not completely dumb!' Tiffany mumbled something else, but Joe kind of flipped.

'Shut up!' he yelled. 'I'm not going to listen to this!' And he turned on his heel and strode past us in the dark. He never even saw us, but for an instant I saw his face flash in the light from the streetlamps. And he was *crying*.

Tiffany got up and walked off crossly in the other direction. Yasmin clung on to my sleeve. 'Wow!' she whispered. 'Wasn't that amazing?!' Yasmin likes rows.

'It wasn't amazing,' I said, shaking her off. 'It was horrid.'

'Let's get back to Froggo,' said Yasmin. I walked fast, slightly ahead of her. I didn't want her to talk about Joe crying.

The others had collected another couple of treats: more sweets. I was sick of sweets. I felt a bit sick in general. Not sick to my stomach exactly. Just upset. There was the trouble with the greenhouse and stuff, for a start, and that was bad enough. But seeing Joe with tears in his eyes was the worst thing to happen for months. I was worried about him, and I actually prayed (silently, of course) that he would be OK.

CHAPTER 14

Wow! Awesome! Amazing!

THE REST OF the evening was OK, but I wasn't really in the mood for it. I ate the supper, I played the games, and I slept with Hannah and Yasmin in Froggo's spare room, in mattresses on the floor. Hannah and Yas did a lot of giggling and stuff before we went off to sleep, but I couldn't concentrate. I just hoped Joe wasn't out somewhere, getting drunk and stealing cars.

Eventually next morning came. Froggo's mum gave us breakfast and drove us home. Dad opened the door to me. He was in his dressing gown. He looked tired. I remembered that they'd had that dinner dance last night.

'How was your night out?' I asked, even though my head was full of other questions. Things I didn't dare mention.

'Fine,' said Dad. 'We danced till Mum's ankle gave out, we ate till we felt sick and we didn't get home till three. And now we've got a pair of prize-winning headaches. I'm just making some tea. Mum's still in bed and she'll be there till lunchtime. I've taken some paracetamol and I'm going to join her in the Intensive Care Unit. You don't mind, do you, Ruby? Shall I make you some toast first?'

'No thanks, Dad,' I said. 'I had breakfast at Dan's.'

Dad disappeared upstairs with a tray. I stood in the kitchen, thinking. This was my chance. If I could creep out into the garden, I could see what had happened to the bottle and the greenhouse – and maybe even clean it up. I knew broken glass could be really dangerous, so I put gloves on.

Quietly I opened the back door and walked down the path. I glanced back up at the house. Joe's bedroom curtains were drawn, so he was definitely still in bed. The other bedroom that overlooks the garden is the spare room. Mum and

Dad's bedroom is at the front of the house, and so is mine. So nobody could see me.

Very carefully, I entered the greenhouse. The bottle had smashed in through one of the panes of glass in the roof. The floor was covered with bits of glass. The bottle had broken too, but the top was intact. You could tell it had been Joe's aftershave. But thank goodness, there was no unusual smell.

I spotted an empty carrier bag from the garden centre and picked it up. Very carefully, and still wearing my gloves, of course, I picked up all the bits of brown glass from Joe's bottle, and put it in the carrier bag. Then I put some of the greenhouse glass in as well.

I noticed an empty cardboard box. It was sort of tall and narrow. The carrier bag fitted into it nicely. I put more glass in, until you couldn't see any brown glass at all, only the clear glass. Then I went back indoors.

I went to my bedroom and played with my monkeys for ages. Then I heard my parents talking and getting up. I went to their room and knocked.

'Come in, love!' called Mum. I went in and sat on the bed. Dad was dressed and combing his hair. Mum was sitting up in bed and looking quite perky.

'There's a pane of glass broken in the greenhouse,' I said. 'I collected all the broken glass with my gloves on and put it in a bag, and the bag's inside a box.'

'Ruby! Whatever did you do that for?' cried Mum. 'You should never touch broken glass. I've told you a hundred times.'

'I was only trying to be helpful,' I said. This was a lie unfortunately. 'Because you weren't feeling well.'

'What were you doing in the greenhouse anyway?' said Mum, shaking her head.

'I thought I'd try and make a den in there,' I said. 'It's nice.'

'She was in there yesterday,' said Dad. 'Under the

staging.' He was backing me up in my treacherous lying ways without even realising it. Poor Dad.

'I don't think a greenhouse is a very suitable place for children to play,' said Mum. 'You've got your tree house. What more do you want?'

'I wonder how the pane of glass got broken in the first place?' Dad was frowning – but not at me. Phew!

'There was a big stone in there,' I said. 'I threw it away.'

'Oh – it was that stupid trick-or-treating, I expect,' said Mum. 'Never mind, Ruby. Dad can soon put another pane of glass in. I'm getting up now. If you want to be useful, go down and unload the dishwasher.'

A few hours later, Joe got up. He looked about as grumpy as anybody has ever been. Mum offered to cook him something, but he said he wasn't hungry. He threw himself down on the sofa and started to watch our DVD of *The Lord of the Rings*.

I brought my monkeys downstairs and I was playing with them on the sitting-room floor. I sort of wanted to keep him company just in case he felt worse with nobody there. Dad was in the greenhouse, and Mum was busy with the chores in the kitchen. I peeped at Joe's face a couple of times. It was blank, as if he wasn't really concentrating.

After a while I felt thirsty and went to the kitchen. Mum was upstairs by now, sorting out the linen. I looked in the fridge. There was a bottle of my favourite juice: orange and raspberry. I took it out. There wasn't much left. I poured out a glassful. It looked lovely. I knew it was going to be delicious.

Suddenly I got an idea. I carried it through to the sitting room and put it down on the coffee table in front of Joe. I didn't say anything. If he didn't want it I could always have it later. Then I got myself a glass of water and went upstairs. I felt *saintly*. It was quite nice after feeling guilty for such a long time.

Later I heard Joe go out. He had drunk the juice, and left the dirty glass on the coffee table. Typical! I left it there too. I'm not *that* saintly. Maybe he'd gone off to make it up with Tiffany. In a funny kind of way, I hoped so. I mean, I don't like her. Compared to Holly she's rubbish. But it had been horrible seeing him crying last night.

I went back upstairs and played with my monkeys. They were planning a bank robbery and they needed my help and advice. They were going to use the money to save the rainforests, obviously, though Stinker did insist that he was also going to buy himself a massive bar of chocolate the size of a sports car.

Round about teatime, I heard Joe come in. He was alone. He came straight upstairs. I expected him to go to his room, slam the door and put loud rock music on, as usual. But he came into my room instead. He didn't knock, but I was too startled to say anything. He was going to accuse me of stealing his aftershave! Oh no!

But wait! He was carrying a box. He started to

climb my stepladder. I got up on to my knees, just in case I needed to hit him or something. He plonked the box down on my mattress.

'I've decided to sort out this stupid fear-of-the-dark thing once and for all,' he said. He crawled into my tree house and opened the box. Guess what?! It was fairy lights! Joe trailed them all among the branches of my tree house. Then he went and got an extension lead and plugged them in. They twinkled like stars.

'Wow!' I said. 'Awesome! Amazing!'

'That's nothing,' said Joe. 'Wait till it's dark. Then they'll look cool.'

He gave me a funny kind of nod, and just went straight out before I even had time to say thank you. He went into his room and started to play his loud rock music. He didn't go out for the rest of the day, and he never mentioned the aftershave. I got the feeling he really had split up with Tiffany. So maybe he didn't need the aftershave any more.

Perhaps once he'd got over Tiffany, he'd feel like going out with somebody else. I hoped so. And if Tiffany wasn't hanging around any more, Holly might come over again. I was keeping my fingers crossed, but I wasn't going to do any of that stupid matchmaking rubbish, like last time.

That night I lay on my sleeping platform under the stars, and imagined I was camping in Africa. And it was amazing, amazing, amazing, amazing, amazing.